This book belongs to:

....

....

For Karsten
C.C.

For David and Alex, I hope you have
lots of great adventures together! x
J.McC.

Reading Consultant: Prue Goodwin, Lecturer in literacy and children's books

ORCHARD BOOKS
338 Euston Road, London NW1 3BH
Orchard Books Australia
Hachette Children's Books
Level 17/207 Kent Street, Sydney NSW 2000

First published in 2011 by Orchard Books
First paperback publication in 2012

Text © Catherine Coe 2011
Illustrations © Jan McCafferty 2011

ISBN 978 1 40830 686 4 (hardback)
ISBN 978 1 40830 694 9 (paperback)

1 3 5 7 9 10 8 6 4 2 (hardback)
1 3 5 7 9 10 8 6 4 2 (paperback)

Printed in China

Orchard Books is a division of Hachette Children's Books,
an Hachette UK company.

www.hachette.co.uk

Showdown
at Dawn

Written by
Catherine Coe

Illustrated by
Jan McCafferty

ORCHARD

Casper the Kid Cowboy just wanted to have fun. His best friend, Pete, agreed. They certainly didn't want any enemies.

But Burt and Bruno had other ideas. They didn't like Pete and Casper one bit.

In fact, Burt and Bruno didn't like *anyone* much. They caused trouble all over town.

In the park . . .

 At the shops . . .

Even outside
the sheriff's
office!

Casper and Pete tried to stay
away from them, but Burt and
Bruno popped up *everywhere*.

Today, they were planning to
cause trouble again.

"Follow me, partner!" Burt said
to Bruno.

"Yee-ha!" Bruno replied.

Casper and Pete were in their treehouse hide-out when they heard a shout from below. Casper looked out, but no one was there.

"That's strange," he said.

Pete stuck his head out to
look, too. "What's that?"
he asked Casper.
There was a piece
of paper stuck to
the tree trunk.

Pete climbed down to grab the
piece of paper. It was a note!

To Casper and Pete,

We challenge you to
a showdown. Meet us
at Lake Ho Ho
at dawn.

From your enemies,
BeB

"It must be Burt and Bruno!" Casper cried. "But we were going to have fun riding our horses tomorrow. I don't want a showdown!"

"It's OK," Pete said calmly.

"We can beat those two!"

Casper wasn't so sure. But Pete
was already preparing for battle.
Their hide-out was full of
useful things.

Then Casper had an idea.
"Whoa there, Pete! What if we
could beat Burt and Bruno before
the showdown even begins?"

"Now *that's* a great idea," Pete said. "Let's make a plan!"

The next day, Casper and
Pete met at their hide-out
before the sun rose.
They each packed a kitbag
and mounted their horses.

Burt and Bruno soon arrived at
Lake Ho Ho. They were excited
about the showdown. But there
was a sign on the gate . . .

Lake Ho Ho
closed for repairs.
Enter at your
own risk.

"Pah," said Burt. "That won't
stop us!"

They leapt over the gate. They were too excited to notice what was waiting for them. The mean pair jumped straight into a big pile of horse manure!

Pete and Casper were hiding
behind a rock, trying not to
laugh out loud.
Burt and Bruno were furious.
They went to wash in the lake.

Casper's plan was working! As the troublemakers turned their backs, he threw his lasso over the smelly pair.

Yee-ha!

"Hey!" Bruno gasped.

23

Burt and Bruno had never been so angry. Pete washed the dirty duo clean.

Meanwhile, Casper got out his secret weapon. His enemies were terrified of spiders!

Burt and Bruno trembled at the sight of the creepy crawlies. "We'll make a deal," Burt said. "Just get those s-s-spiders away from us!"

Argh!

Casper turned to Pete. "Do you
think we should let them go?"

"No way, partner," said Pete.
"Unless . . ."
"What? We'll do anything!"
Bruno yelled.

Casper and Pete decided to
teach their enemies a lesson.
In the park, Burt and Bruno
had to pick up litter.

At the shops,
they had to
give all their
sweets away.

And at the sheriff's office,
they had to groom the horses.
Being tied together made
everything much harder!

As the sun set, Casper and Pete decided Burt and Bruno had done enough.

The two troublesome cowboys might be nicer from now on. And if not, Casper and Pete knew what to do!

Tomorrow, the two best friends would be able to have fun again – without any enemies to worry about!

Written by **Illustrated by**
Catherine Coe **Jan McCafferty**

All priced at £8.99

Orchard Books are available from all good bookshops,
or can be ordered from our website: www.orchardbooks.co.uk,
or telephone 01235 827702, or fax 01235 827703.

Prices and availability are subject to change.